PORTLAND AND THE SNOWFLAKE

FANESIA HEATH

SkyLightBooks

An imprint of Tandem Light Press

Skylight Books
an imprint of Tandem Light Press
950 Herrington Rd.
Suite C128
Lawrenceville, GA 30044

Tandem Light Press paperback edition November 2016
ISBN: 978-0-9861660-4-4
Library of Congress Control Number: 2015936140

Biblical passages are from the King James Bible

PRINTED IN THE UNITED STATES OF AMERICA

I would like to dedicate this book to my father, Allen L. Green, who has always told me that one day, I will write a book.

Dad, with this book in my hands, nothing but tears flows from my eyes, for I know you knew it would come. I just wish you were here to hold it with me. I miss you so much. You fought a good fight, but Heaven needed your laughs and your personality. I know you are proud. I dedicate my first book to you, Daddy. Rest well. I love and miss you dearly!

"We are all a little weird and life's a little weird and when we find someone whose weirdness is compatible with ours, we join up with them and fall in mutual weirdness and call it love."

-Dr. Seuss

ACKNOWLEDGMENTS

I would like to thank God for choosing to gift me with this creative mind and the ability to put words into a story.

I am so thankful for the parents who raised me to be a strong woman. Rhonda and Allen Green, I never stop hearing those words spoken to me: "Never stop writing." The push you gave me alongside my sister and my brother, Martina and Rory Green, to always better myself.

Above all, I would like to thank Willie Heath who has been my rock and to my four growing hands who call me "mommy": Kayla, Brison, Zyon, and Amir who have encouraged me through this journey.

I want to say a huge thank you to Andie Baker who introduced me to an inspiring author, Yolanda Harris, who helped guide me by passing the torch to me to continue in my journey. Thank you to my close family and friends who established the resources to start my dream. To all my close family and friends who have held my hand through the long phone calls, meetings, and lunch dates while listening to my dreams.

I would also like to say thank you to the pastor and leaders from the start who told me writing a book would be my mission. The ladies in my journey group and support from my church family at CrossPoint City Church has been wonderful.

Saving these two amazing women last, who have believed in me and been so supportive from the day we started my journey: my publisher, Dr. Pamela, and my editor, Ms. Caroline. Thank you so much for allowing me this opportunity to live out my dreams in the books I write.

We're expecting snow today! My mama said as soon as it begins to snow that I can go outside and play. The clouds are heavy as I sit looking out my living room window waiting for the first flake to fall. My mama gave me paper and crayons to draw out the snowman that I want to build.

Mama is in the kitchen as she yells over the running sink water, "Ladybug, do you want to help me bake cookies while you wait for the snow to come?"

"No, ma'am not right now." As much as I want to bake cookies, I am more excited about the snow coming so I can build my snowman. I don't want to pull myself away from the window.

I turn on the TV to watch the weatherman and hear how close the snow is to my town. He says, "Ten minutes to Sugar village."

"That's us!" I yell out loud.

I quickly run to my room to dress warmly and prepare for the snow.

Mama peeks in, "Portland, make sure you put on two coats. It's very cold outside and the wind is blowing, so make sure you cover your head and your hands. I'd suggest you put on your favorite matching hat and gloves before you go play."

After I'm dressed, I run to my swing set to swing and wait for the snow to fall. I sway back and forth looking up at the gray clouds and my purple watch.

I become more and more tired from just waiting. Minutes have passed, but in my mind I think it has been hours. As I start to head back into the house, I feel a cold, wet drop fall onto my forehead. I look up and see lots of snowflakes falling on the ground. I open my mouth to catch as many as I can on my tongue.

The snow is falling down as if the sprinklers are on! I spread my arms, run in circles, and jump up and down joyfully. I scream out to my mom: "The snow is beautiful, Mama!"

Mama comes to the front door. She watches me spin around in circles with my arms outstretched and my mouth open wide. She has a huge smile on her face.

The snow is starting to cover up my shoes and the grass. I reach down and grab a handful of snow, throwing it up into the air, and run through it screaming "Yippee! Yippee!" I cry out loud into the cold winter air, then fall on my back spreading my arms out like angel wings. Snow angels make me so happy.

Suddenly, I feel a large snowflake hit my nose and bounce off. I sit up to get a better look at the snowflake. I jump up to follow it. The snowflake is not like all snowflakes; it's large with a very unique shape.

Excited to see where the snowflake will float away to, I look back at the house. Mama has gone back to doing chores, I follow after this snowflake, not knowing how far it will float. I have to know why this snowflake is so different than any other snowflake.

Pulling my hat and gloves on tighter to keep warm, I struggle to keep up with the snowflake in the deep snow. The wind begins to blow harder, making the sight of the snowflake difficult for me to see

As I walk faster and climb small hills, I manage to keep my eyes on the snowflake. With all the walking I've done, I think to myself that I'm many miles away from home. I didn't mean to walk so far.

I start to notice that the snowflake is drifting to the park right across from my house. The park my parents visit every other day. "I have to slow down," I say, breathing rapidly trying to catch my breath. I reach out my arms to lean on a huge oak tree. I look ahead to see where the snowflake went and see it resting on a leaf.

I see a little girl lying on a bench under the tree. I don't speak because I'm afraid if I do I'll frighten her. I look around to see if I can find her parents.

"Excuse me," I say softly. She jumps up, frightened.

"Yes? Do I know you?" she asks me, shivering.

"I don't think so. I'm Portland. I live around the corner. Silly to say, but I followed this huge snowflake and we ended up here."

I notice she looks cold with no coat. I take off my jacket and give it to her. "Glad I have two jackets on," I smile. We both giggle as we zip up our jackets to keep warm.

"So what's your name and why are you here at this park alone without your parents?"

With her head down she replies, "I'm here because I also followed a unique snowflake and it led me here too. I lost it. I got tired and found this blanket. I laid down and must have fallen asleep. My name is Snow." She laughs out loud and says, "I know it's very unique and perfect for this day.

We start talking and learning more about each other and that we attend the same school. I learn she has had little to no friends because she is so shy.

"I don't have any friends either," " I say, "because they all think it's weird to pray. I pray over my lunch, and for this person who is very mean to me every day. But I've learned to never give up, to follow my heart, and to share love no matter how big or small."

Snow replies back "Portland! That's how I feel! Praying gives me comfort like this blanket and jacket on a cold day, or food for the squirrels to put away. God is always there with us each and every day, to help us meet someone who understands how we feel, and show us that there are others like us; special and real."

So my new friend and I begin to play. "Let's build this snowman that I have in mind," I said, "He's going to be different and stand out from all the other ones that are being built today. We'll build him with love and dress him with faith and finish him off together."

We start to roll our snowball together and before too long we're done and noticing that the daylight is coming to an end. We've had the best snow day in the park and we agree that it's time to get back home before our parents get worried about us.

The snowflake that we were both following didn't reappear. Snow says to me, "Maybe it's time had come and it melted away."

I hug Snow and say goodbye. She hands me back my coat, then we head in opposite directions. I start to talk to God about my day how it all started with a snowflake. I pause in my footsteps and finally figure it out. With smaller snowflakes falling on my face, I smile up at God, "Thank you for bringing the unique snowflake my way that lead me to the park to meet my new friend. Snow is nice and loves snow and has a unique story to tell just like me!"

When I get to my driveway, I still have a huge smile on my face. I skip towards the front door. I look up and see the night is painting the sky and the stars are getting into place.

I fly though the front door, "Mom!" I shout, "I have to tell you about my day! It was exciting and unique, and I met someone named Snow."

Mama chuckles and says, "I know, sweetheart, you met a lot of it today."

After my bath, mama tucks me into bed ready to listen to all I have to say. I tell her about my day being out in the snow and seeing a unique snowflake and being lead to meet Snow as I played.

Mama leans over and gives me a kiss on my forehead. She smiles, looks at me, and says, "That's what I love about you, your imagination and how much you enjoyed playing in the snow today."

Then I ask mom if we can go to the park tomorrow and play with all the other kids.

"I guess so," she says with a grin. "We'll have to make sure we take extra clothes, gloves, and even pack a basket of food just in case."

As I hug my mom tight, I look up to God again and say, "Thank you again for my snowflake because it led me to meet someone just like me: a seven-year-old, who loves you and shares love the same way. Goodnight."

ABOUT THE AUTHOR

Fanesia Heath wears many hats as a daughter, sister, aunt, and as a friend and wife of nine years and a mother to four children. She has one princess and three princes. Writing has been her passion since middle school. It was where she could put her dreams, testimonies, and experiences into words and tell a story. In addition to writing, Ms. Heath is an accomplished volleyball player. Being a working mom of four has taught her that no matter what may blow your way, allow it to be a lesson to learn or a reason for the moment.

CPSIA information can be obtained
at www.ICGtesting.com
Printed in the USA
LVOW06s2329151216
517513LV00013B/48/P

9 780986 166044